Text copyright © Sally Grindley 1999
Illustrations copyright © Tania Hurt-Newton 1999

First published in Great Britain in 1999
by Macdonald Young Books
an imprint of Wayland Publishers Ltd
61 Western Road
Hove
East Sussex
BN3 1JD

Find Macdonald Young Books on the internet at
http://www.myb.co.uk

Printed in Hong Kong by Wing King Tong

British Library Cataloguing in Publication Data available

ISBN 0 7500 2754 1

SALLY GRINDLEY

# Mulberry
## alone at the seaside

Illustrated by Tania Hurt-Newton

MACDONALD YOUNG BOOKS

Mulberry sat on the beach and wagged
his tail.
"Shall we play ball?" he barked.
"Lie down, Mulberry," they said.
"Shall we go in the water?" he barked.

"Be quiet, Mulberry, we're having a rest."
Mulberry put his head on his paws.
"I don't want to lie down," he growled,
"I want to play."

Nobody moved.
Then I'll play on my own, he thought.

He trotted down to look at the sea.
Mulberry had never seen the sea before.
It was big and noisy and he wasn't sure
that he liked it.
Mulberry put one paw in the water.

Mulberry put two paws in the water.
Then he jumped right in and began to
doggy-paddle.

Suddenly, a big wave broke over him
and Mulberry had a mouthful of sea.

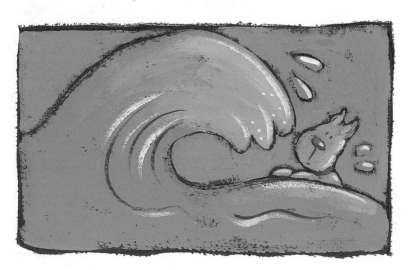

YUK! It tasted horrible!
Mulberry ran out of the sea.

He trotted off along the beach.
"Hello," he barked, "I'm Mulberry.
Does anyone want to play?"
A girl was digging in the sand.
Mulberry liked digging.

He rushed over and knocked down
the sand-castle the girl had just made.

Then he started to dig.
"Aren't I clever?" he barked.
The girl started to cry.
Mulberry heard cross voices.
"Bad dog, you've spoilt her sand-castle."

Mulberry didn't like cross voices,
so he ran away.

Mulberry saw a ball rolling down
the beach towards the sea.
"Mulberry to the rescue," barked
Mulberry.

He grabbed the ball in his jaws and
held it in the air.

A boy ran towards him.
Mulberry dropped the ball.
"Let's play!" he barked.
He picked up the ball again and
ran along the beach.
The boy chased after him.

"Give me back my ball," shouted
the boy.
Mulberry stopped and dropped it.

The boy reached for the ball, but
Mulberry grabbed it again and
ran off.

Suddenly, the ball went all floppy.
"He's burst my ball!" yelled the boy.
Mulberry heard cross voices behind him.

He dropped the ball and ran away
as fast as he could.

Now Mulberry felt hungry.
"It's time to eat," he barked loudly.
He sniffed – SNIFF! – and again –
SNIFF! and he smelt a tasty smell.
He saw some towels stretched out on
the sand. He saw a bag beside the towels.

Mulberry sniffed his way over to the
bag. He put his nose in and pulled out
a sausage roll.
"Yum, yum!" he barked as he gobbled it
down. He put his nose in the bag again
and pulled out a chicken sandwich.

Mulberry heard voices.
"Stop that dog!"
Mulberry pulled his nose out of the bag.
Cross feet were running across the sand
towards him.

Cross voices were shouting at him.
Mulberry didn't like cross voices.
"Have I been naughty?" he whimpered
and he ran away as fast as he could.

When Mulberry stopped running,
he saw rocks in front of him.
"I'll go climbing," he barked.
He leapt from one rock to another.

In between the rocks there were
pools of water. Mulberry put his paw
in one of the rock pools and moved
some seaweed. A crab looked up at him.
Mulberry tried to sniff it. The crab
pinched him on the nose.

Mulberry jumped and the crab fell
back into the rock pool.

Now Mulberry felt tired.
He found a large, flat rock
and lay down on it in the sunshine.
Soon he was fast asleep.

When he woke up, the sun had gone
in and it was getting cold.
"Time to go back," barked Mulberry.
He trotted back over the rocks. They
were slippery. Then Mulberry saw that
the sea was all round the rocks.

A wave smashed against the rocks and splashed Mulberry.
"Stop that," he growled.
Another wave smashed against the rocks and splashed Mulberry.
A huge wave crashed against the rocks and soaked Mulberry.

"I want to go home," he howled.
"I want my doggy basket and my
chewy bone and my squeaky ball."
He scrambled over the rocks to
the cliffs and found a cave.
Mulberry peered inside.

It was cold and dark inside the cave.
Drops of water dripped on to
Mulberry's nose.

Then Mulberry saw a light in the distance. He began to run towards it, faster and faster.

The light grew bigger and bigger until suddenly Mulberry found himself back on the beach.

"Mulberry," he heard. "Mulberry, where are you?"
Mulberry pricked up his ears.
"Here I am," he barked loudly.

He ran towards the voices, and there they were, full of hugs and kind words. "I'm so pleased to see you," he barked.

They walked back along the beach
and Mulberry stayed close by.
He didn't dig in the sand.
He didn't chase any balls.
He didn't look back at the sea.

Mulberry had had enough of the
seaside for one day.

Look out for more of Mulberry's adventures:

## Mulberry Alone in the Park by Sally Grindley

The front door has been left open. It must be doggy walkies time for Mulberry. So off he trots to the park. He has great fun chasing squirrels and doggy-paddling after the ducks. But then it starts to get dark. Mulberry is woken by a loud bang, then another. Bright colours light up the sky. Maybe being alone in the park is not such fun after all...

## Mulberry Home Alone by Sally Grindley

Mulberry the dog doesn't like being home alone. But he tries to make the best of it. First he searches for his doggy crunchy things. Whoops! He's knocked over the rubbish bin. Then he decides to chase Cat. Whoops! He's crashed into the telephone table. Luckily, Mulberry isn't home alone for long.

## Mulberry Alone on the Farm by Sally Grindley

Mulberry visits a farm for the day. He runs off to look for someone to play with, but the hens, the piglets and the scarecrow don't want to play with him. Mulberry is fed up, until the sky grows dark and he gets caught in a scary thunderstorm.

All these books in the Mulberry series can be purchased from your local bookseller. For more information about Mulberry, write to: *The Sales Department, Macdonald Young Books, 61 Western Road, Hove, East Sussex BN3 1JD*